Magnolias In Bloom

By Debby Mayne

Copyright © Deborah Mayne 2015
Forget Me Not Romances, a division of Winged Publications

All rights reserved. No part of this publication may be reproduced, stored in a retrieval system, or transmitted in any form or by any means, with the exception of brief quotations in printed reviews.

This book is a work of fiction. The characters in this story are the product of the author's imagination and are completely fictitious.

ISBN-13: 978-1547122806
ISBN-10: 1547122803

Chapter 1

As Amelia Sawyer approached the long driveway flanked by magnolia trees in full bloom, the familiar blend of family coziness and protection flooded her, as well as the restrictive boundaries her parents still imposed, even though she'd finished college and worked as a teacher for several years. She loved the old home that had been in her family for three generations, but she didn't miss the constant hovering and worries from her parents. That was why she'd moved into her own apartment immediately after college. She told her parents she wanted to be closer to the school where she taught, but in reality, she wanted to come and go without having to answer to anyone, especially her meddlesome mother who meant well but stressed her out.

The fragrance of the magnolias sent all of her senses reeling. She loved spring in Biloxi. This was the time of year when everything was greener, most of the flowers budded out, and the magnolias held court over everything. They definitely took over, both with their intense, sweet fragrance and the large white blooms that caught the eye of anyone whose eyes were open. Amelia remembered her school days during the late spring with a combination of fondness and dread. She loved the idea that summer was near, but she dreaded the blistering hot days that followed. Another thing the magnolias reminded her of was her parents' unending reminders that all of this would be hers eventually, and they wanted her to find a man and settle down. She totally wasn't ready for that now ... and maybe not ever. Although she enjoyed coming home for a little while, this wasn't what she wanted in life. It was too restricting. But it still provided a cushion she needed at times like this.

She pulled up in front of the house on the circular driveway right behind a large pickup truck with *Hawkins Homes* in block lettering on the sides and got out. Mama had told her they were restoring some of the trim in the house to bring it back to its historical glory and renovating the kitchen to give it a more contemporary feel.

The familiar aroma of cinnamon mixed with lemon spray enveloped her as she entered the mansion her great-grandfather had built with the money he'd made from his local chain of hardware stores. He'd started out as a handyman, saved his money, and eventually opened a small store in downtown Biloxi. His gregarious manner had people flocking to his business, so it wasn't long before he opened his second and third stores in Gulfport and Long Beach. He continued to expand, but eventually, he sold the less profitable stores but kept the ones that provided well for his family as well as the people he employed. He left a dozen Sawyer Hardware stores to Amelia's grandfather who eventually expanded farther north, all the way to Jackson.

"Hi there." The sound of a man's voice captured her attention.

She spun around and found herself face-to-face with a dark-haired man with brooding eyes. He was more rugged than traditionally handsome, but he had a face that commanded attention. And the way he looked at her gave her heart a little flutter. She lifted her chin, hoping he wouldn't see the effect he had on her. "Hi. Who are you?"

He wiped his hand on his faded jeans and extended it. "Logan Hawkins." He grinned, exposing a near-perfect smile as they shook hands. "I assume you're the daughter with the flooded apartment."

"Assumptions aren't good," she replied. "But yes, I'm that daughter."

"It's nice to meet you." He continued studying her.

She finally stepped to the side and pointed toward the back of the house. "Well, I need to go find my mother."

"She's in the kitchen waiting for you." He let out a soft chuckle before he turned toward the dining room, leaving her standing there, staring after him.

Something about Logan Hawkins made her uncomfortable, maybe partly because she found him immensely attractive—even more so as she continued talking to him. His expressive face and deep voice gave him a commanding presence that resonated as nothing else ever had. As soon as she got to the kitchen, her mother did a double take.

"What's got you in such a dither?" her mother asked.

"I'm not in a dither." Before her mother could continue asking questions, Amelia decided to change the topic. "What all are you having done to the kitchen?"

"Everything." She pointed as she continued. "New appliances, new countertop, resurfaced cabinets, relocating the island. Anything that doesn't look fresh is being changed, and like I said, that covers pretty much everything."

"Mama, have you been watching home renovation shows again?"

"Well ..." Her mother offered a sheepish smile. "Yes. But that's a good thing. I get to see a lot of different styles, and now I know what I want." She waved toward the exact same refrigerator that had been in the exact same spot for as long as Amelia could remember. "Pour yourself a glass of sweet tea, and I'll tell you what I've been thinking."

"Okay, but I don't want to wait too long to bring

my stuff in."

"Is your car parked out front?"

Amelia nodded. "I pulled in behind the renovation guy's truck."

"You're talking about Logan. Why don't I ask if he can bring your stuff in for you?" Her mother sighed. "He's such a nice young man. Maybe the two of you can—"

"No."

"Don't be snappy, Amelia. You don't even know what I was going to say."

"Okay, what were you going to say?" Amelia lifted an eyebrow and gave her mother a look that used to earn her an extended trip to her room.

"I was thinking that since he's single, and you're single …" Her mother held her hands out, palms up. "Maybe y'all can go out—"

Amelia shook her head. "That's what I thought, and the answer is still no. I don't need anyone to find men for me."

"You don't exactly have them lining up to meet you, and it's not like you're not pretty or smart enough. You have to make time … make an effort." Her mother leaned forward and looked her in the eyes as she always did to make sure Amelia got her point. "If you'd just slow down and get to know him, I'm sure y'all will get along just fine."

"Maybe so, but at the moment, I'm too busy to slow down."

"That's your problem. You stay on-the-go all the time, and before you know it, your entire life will flash by, and you'll be a sad, lonely, old woman." She made a face. "No husband, no kids, no house. Just you and your projects."

Amelia couldn't help but laugh. "I'm twenty-five years old. I think I have plenty of time left before you can call me an old maid."

"I never called you an old maid."

"But that's what you implied, which tells me what you were thinking." Amelia cleared her throat. "So tell me more about your plans for the kitchen."

Her mother closed her eyes and shook her head before finally letting out a deep sigh of resignation. "These cabinets are original wood, and they're in good shape, so I thought I'd just have them painted. We'll add nice hardware too, of course."

"Yes, of course."

Amelia's mother gave her a curious look but continued. "This island is too small, so I thought I'd have a larger one designed and put it in the center of the kitchen. There's plenty of space that's not getting used. It'll be perfect for two people cooking together. In fact, it would be romantic for a couple to make a nice dinner together. Don't you think that would be nice?"

"Absolutely." Amelia thought back and couldn't come up with a single time her parents cooked together.

"And we'd get all brand new appliances. Your daddy said he'd like black appliances, but that's not what I want."

"You're the one who spends more time in the kitchen, so I think you should get what you want," Amelia said.

"I agree." The voice came from the doorway, snagging the attention of both Amelia and her mother. "You said you preferred stainless, and I think that would be perfect with the hardware you've picked out for the cabinets."

"See? I told you how nice he was."

It took everything Amelia had not to roll her eyes. Anytime someone agreed with her mother, she thought they were nice.

"Come on in, Logan." Her mother stood. "Have a seat, and I'll get you some tea."

"No thanks. I just wanted to let you know that you need to go ahead and decide between the granite and quartz. We have to order it soon, and it'll take several weeks for it to arrive."

"Oh dear." Amelia's mother turned to her. "Which do you think I should pick? Granite or quartz?"

"I don't even know the difference. Choose whichever one you like better."

"It's so hard to decide. I like both of them, and your father isn't helping at all. He said that since I'm being so stubborn about the appliances, the kitchen is mine to decorate. Unfortunately, the more I look at them online, the harder it is to choose." Before Amelia had a chance to say anything, her mother's eyes lit up. "Hey, I have an idea. Why don't the two of you go look at both and help me decide?"

Logan turned to Amelia. "I don't know."

"I don't think so." Amelia didn't want Logan to be put on the spot. "After I get all my stuff in my old room, I have to leave."

Her mother frowned. "I wasn't talking about right now. Maybe in the next day or so."

"I'm sure he's busy." Amelia had to cut her mom off from such thoughts, or she'd wind up having a date every night while she stayed in the house.

"But when you get home from school and he finishes up for the day—"

"I'm involved with an important project every single day." She shot Logan an apologetic look. "Maybe you can pick one without me."

A look of amusement passed over his face as he turned to her mom. "I'm afraid I don't want to make this decision for you. You might not be happy with what I pick."

Amelia turned to her mother. "Mama, he's right. You're the one who needs to pick what you like."

"What if I make a mistake? I've never done this before."

"You won't make a mistake if it's what you want."

Her mother closed her eyes and shook her head. "When I first started with this project, I thought it would be so easy. After all, I hired the best company for the job." She momentarily smiled at Logan, but the smile faded when she turned to Amelia. "But it's turning out to be much more daunting that I ever imagined."

"Mrs. Sawyer, you've done an excellent job so far. If you'd like me to, I can bring some granite and quartz samples here, but it won't be the same as seeing the whole slab."

She nodded. "At least I can narrow it down before I go to the showroom and look at the slabs. It'll be a whole lot easier than looking at thousands of them and having to make a decision there."

"Thousands?" Amelia challenged.

"You know what I mean. Hundreds."

"Then it's settled." Logan backed toward the door. "I'll bring some samples to the house, and you can pick several that you want to see when you go to the shop." He did a mock salute. "I'll see you ladies later."

After he left, Amelia's mother turned all of her attention to Amelia. "Why don't you want to go out with Logan? He's a perfectly nice man."

"I'm sure he is, but ..." She swallowed hard. "You know how busy I am."

"I know you hate when I do this, but you really need to stop being so busy with your causes and let some nice young man into your life. How do you ever expect to find Mr. Right if you keep running around doing charity work during your free time?"

"I like what I do, Mama. Who's to say I won't meet him during one of my missions? Besides, I'll be fine if I never meet Mr. Right. My life is exactly how I want it."

"That's what I used to say before I met your

daddy. I had a nice job working at the department store, where I got a very nice discount. When they promoted me, I thought I had the world by the tail."

Amelia had heard this story many times, but she wasn't about to call her mother out on it. "That was different, though. You met Daddy doing what you both enjoyed doing."

"How do you know you and Logan don't both enjoy the same things?"

"Tell you what, Mama. If I run into Logan at the soup kitchen or the food bank or even in that house we're building for the latest family in the Christian Partnership, I'll think about getting to know him better."

Her mother closed her eyes and rubbed her temples. "I worry about you, Amelia. I don't want you to wake up one day and wonder how your life got away from you."

*

All the way home, Logan tried to erase Amelia Sawyer's image from his mind. She was not only cute she had that spunk he'd always found so attractive in women. He liked her mother too, but he felt bad about the obvious strain between them.

Logan's dad had warned him early in life about women with minds of their own. His mantra had been *You're better off alone than with a woman who has her own agenda*. Logan knew that was directly due to the fact that his mother had left him and his dad early in his life, and she only showed up when she felt like it, which wasn't very often. She was as busy as Amelia's mother said she was, but for her, it was all about chasing the dollar. Anything she did or thought deserved her time had money attached to it.

When Logan was a little boy, he missed his mother, but over time, he grew accustomed to living without her. The times she made an appearance, he couldn't get enough of her, but he knew she'd be gone soon, so he kept his emotional distance.

As time went on, he came to understand some things about his dad. He wasn't the easiest person to live with, and although he never tipped the bottle in front of Logan, he was often tipsy. Fortunately, he wasn't a mean drunk. But unfortunately, there were times when Logan had to be the adult and make decisions that weren't always the best ones. But he'd learned from his mistakes, so when he moved out, he was prepared to take care of himself.

In spite of what his dad said, Logan liked women who knew what they wanted and went for it. He found that sense of purpose very attractive.

He grinned as he pulled up in front of the old house he'd purchased with the intention of remodeling exactly how he wanted it. He still hadn't done much besides paint, but he wasn't in any rush. He'd eventually get around to doing it, one project at a time.

After eating leftovers from dinner the night

before with his former next-door neighbors who'd first brought him to church when he was a teenager, he got in bed and read until his eyelids grew heavy. Then he turned off the light and fell fast asleep.

He awoke with a smile on his face that was most likely prompted by his dream of Amelia. She'd clearly had an impact on him because in his dream, they worked alongside each other, hammering nails in a house for one of the local families. As he propped up on his elbows, he decided that if any part of his dream ever did come true, he'd consider dating Amelia, even though that wasn't something that was likely to happen. The projects he was involved with demanded an immense amount of mental and physical grunt work, not something a southern belle raised in an old Biloxi mansion would likely want to get into.

He got out of bed and started the coffee maker. Before he had a chance to get dressed, his phone rang. It was Mrs. Sawyer.

"Hey, Logan, I know it's early, but can you come early today?"

"Um ..." He glanced at the clock and saw that it wasn't even 7:00 AM yet. "Is there an emergency?"

"Sort of." The tone of her voice didn't sound stressed or worried, but he took her for her word. "Let me throw on some clothes, and I'll be right over."

Chapter 2

"You did what?" Amelia glared at her mother who'd just confessed to calling Logan.

"Calm down, sweetie. He was planning to come anyway, but I wanted to make sure you were still here when he arrived. I know how you like to pack your Saturdays with one activity after another."

Amelia opened her mouth, but she was so frustrated nothing would come out. Her mother had schemed before, but this really took the cake. She just sank down in the kitchen chair and buried her face in her hands.

"Come on, Amelia, please listen to me." She smiled. "Please humor me this once. He's such a sweet man, and you've seen how kind and nice looking he is. I just want to make it easy for y'all to get to know each other, so I'm opening up some opportunities."

Amelia couldn't help but laugh. "Opportunities?

More like desperate attempts at matchmaking if you ask me."

Her mother shrugged. "Maybe, but seriously, what is wrong with matchmaking? That's how your daddy and I got together. Some smart family members thought we'd get along, and they were right. Now it's my turn to pay it forward."

Amelia gave her mother a comical look. "I don't think that's what is meant by paying it forward."

"Oh, but I think it is." Her mother smiled and patted her on the shoulder. "I need to go put on some lipstick before Logan gets here. He should be here any minute."

If Amelia thought she could go now and get away with it, she would. But she still had a few things to do around the house before leaving for the day.

"I'll be in my room." Amelia got up and walked to the door and then stopped, turned around, and waited for her mother to look at her. "I have a lot to do today, and I probably won't be home until after supper."

"You won't be here for supper?" She heard the pain in her mother's voice. "But I thought—" She stopped abruptly and let out a longsuffering sigh. "Okay, that's fine. I just thought it would be fun for the family to have supper together."

"Just the family?" Amelia lifted an eyebrow and tilted her head as she held her mother's gaze.

Her mother sheepishly glanced away. "Well, maybe a guest or two."

Amelia chuckled. "That's what I thought. Go ahead and invite your guests. Without me, there'll be more food for the rest of you."

"But Amelia—" Her mother stopped before continuing her argument and pursed her lips. "Okay."

With that, Amelia turned and went to her room. Fortunately, she'd already scheduled herself to work at the soup kitchen, and after everyone was served, she was supposed to go to the food bank at the church to help sort canned items. And then she planned to stop by the house the Christian Partnership was working on for one of the families they supported so she could lend a hand there.

Yes, she realized she filled her day with activities, but it beat sitting around worrying about some guy, like her best friend since high school Chelsea did. She'd managed to talk Chelsea into joining her in some of her charity work, but after one full day, Chelsea said she hated every minute of it. She was better at visiting the elderly in their homes and reading Bible passages.

The two of them had met in church at the beginning of seventh grade. They went to different middle schools, but they went to the same high school. From their first chat on the phone, they became the best of friends—not so much because they had much in common but because they didn't. They both tried out for cheerleader and made the squad. Chelsea was one of the girls at the base of the pyramid, while Amelia was the girl at the very top—the girl who did a double flip off the pyramid and landed on her feet … most of the time. And that's how they were as friends. Chelsea played it safe and did what was expected of her, providing stability and saneness, while Amelia took risks. Except with guys.

"Amelia!"

The sound of her mother calling her name from the base of the stairs bothered her. "I'll be down in a minute."

Her mother didn't respond. When Amelia opened her bedroom door, she heard voices—her mother's and a man's—at the base of the stairs. She listened for a moment and decided it didn't sound like Logan.

She stuffed her hairbrush, makeup bag, sneakers, and change of clothes into a tote before going downstairs to say goodbye to her mother, who'd probably try to stall her until Logan arrived. But she didn't plan to wait around.

"Hey, Mama, I'm going—" She stopped as soon as she spotted a man she'd never seen before standing in the kitchen chatting with her mother. "Oh, hi." She turned to her mother. "I'll see you around eight or nine."

"Wait a minute, sweetie. I want you to meet Logan's assistant who'll be doing some work around here today since Logan had something else he needed to do."

"But I thought you said he was coming."

"He did come, but he had to run." She turned

toward the man. "He just stopped by to introduce me to this nice young man."

Amelia smiled at the guy and extended her hand. "I'm Amelia Sawyer."

The guy in front of her looked her in the eyes and shook her hand. "Nice to meet you, Amelia. I'm Brandon." Instead of letting go, he held onto her hand for an extra second—long enough to get a scowl from her mother.

She pulled her hand back. "Nice to meet you too. I hate to be rude, but I'm supposed to be somewhere in a few minutes."

Brandon continued to hold her gaze as his eyelids fell slightly, giving her an odd sensation that he saw something in her that no one else did. He was handsome but a little too boyish for her taste. As soon as she realized where her thoughts had gone, she cleared her throat and turned around, waving over her shoulder.

She was both startled and annoyed by her disappointment of not seeing Logan. What did it matter that he took off before she got downstairs and left his assistant? He was just there to do a job, and besides, she wouldn't even be in the house most of the day.

All the way to the soup kitchen, Amelia tried to steer her thoughts away from Logan and the way his image lingered in her mind long after she was around him. But that was impossible because the effort of trying to force him from her thoughts backfired and did the exact opposite.

When she finally arrived at the soup kitchen, she got out of her car, ran through the parking lot, and entered the work area through the back door. Stan, the guy in charge of her group, lifted a spoon in greeting and grinned. "Take over at the ovens. We have biscuits and apple turnovers today."

Amelia did as she was told and immediately became immersed in her soup kitchen duties. After all the food was done, she helped set it up for the people who'd come in to serve. Once the clients got their food and started eating, she walked around the dining hall to make sure everyone had what they needed before she left for the food bank her church was involved with.

The food bank always received a large load of canned goods from the local grocery stores late on Friday, so Saturdays were mostly spent sorting the varieties. She loved the mindless task of putting cans of green beans in one box and creamed corn in another. After everything was sorted, she often stuck around to fill the boxes to hand out to families, but she'd already told Andrew, the jobsite foreman at the Christian Partnership construction site, that she'd help with some of the finishing touches on the house they were working on now. The family was running out of time before they had to be out of their rental, and they needed their home soon.

Fortunately, there were enough volunteers at the food bank to fill the boxes, so she said goodbye to the other volunteers and took off for the construction site. As soon as she pulled into the parking lot where there were more than a dozen cars and trucks, she got out of her car, popped her trunk, changed shoes, put on her hardhat, and headed toward the house that was close to move-in ready.

She felt that familiar tickling in her tummy at the thought of being a part of such a worthy project. Nothing was more important in the world than helping a family who loved the Lord and tried really hard to make ends meet.

Although Amelia had never had to struggle financially, she'd been around plenty of folks who lost everything because of a lack of jobs, health issues, storms, or some unexpected devastating event. One of her friends in high school had lost her mother in a car accident, and her dad was so depressed he turned to the bottle. Within a couple of years, he lost his job, they lost their house, and Linea had to move to Louisiana to live with her grandparents because her father was incapable of being a parent.

Amelia's parents offered to let her stay with them, but Linea's father's pride was too strong. After Linea left town, Amelia still had Chelsea, but what had happened to her affected her views on everything, and she soon discovered that Linea's situation wasn't isolated. There were quite a few people who experienced life-changing tragedies. At times she even felt guilty about all of her blessings. That was when she started pouring all her energy into helping those who were less fortunate. Her mother tried to convince her she didn't need to feel guilty, but she did.

On top of that, she still really missed Linea. They still had long phone conversations, but there were times when it would have been nice to sit across from each other over a plate of brownies and tall glasses of milk like they used to. They'd talked about getting together after they finished school, but Linea had run out of money, so she dropped out of college and joined the Air Force. Although she still did things with Chelsea on occasion, Amelia realized that she needed balance with her friends. So she embraced these missions and made friends with the people who had the same passion for serving the less fortunate. At some point, she realized her passion had turned into an obsession.

As Amelia approached the house, she looked around at everyone working hard at putting the finishing touches on the house. "Has anyone seen Andrew?" she asked the group painting the front porch.

One of the guys pointed to the door. "He's been looking for you. Said he has a special project just for you. I think he's in the kitchen."

"Special project?"

The guy shrugged. "No idea what it is, but he specifically mentioned you by name." He paused. "You are Amelia, aren't you?"

She nodded. She'd met most of the people on the crew, but there were so many of them who came and went, she couldn't remember all of their names.

Last time she was in this house, her task was to put the hardware on the kitchen cabinets. She glanced around when she got to the door of the kitchen and smiled. It was starting to look really nice—like a kitchen she'd want if she ever bought a house.

"Hey Amelia. I heard you were going to be here today."

She spun around at the sound of the familiar voice and found herself face-to-face with someone she didn't expect. "Logan?"

Chapter 3

He folded his arms and smiled back at her. "When I told Andrew I'd sent someone else to work on your parents' house so I could be here, he asked if I wanted to partner with you. I figured that since your folks were looking at countertops and backsplashes, we could kill two birds with one stone."

Amelia narrowed her eyes. "I'm not here to kill birds."

Logan chuckled. "Okay, we'll let them live, but we still need to find something inexpensive but nice for this house. While we're there, we can get the samples for you to take home for your mother to look at."

"While we're where?"

Andrew chose that moment to approach. "I see you found each other. Logan and I were just talking about the—"

"She knows. I just told her." Logan turned to her. "How about it? Are you ready to go look at some kitchen materials?" He paused. "We need to pick up some things for this house. That's the other bird I was talking about."

She laughed. "Sure. Let's go."

Once they got to his truck, she turned to him. "When did you start working for Christian Partnership?"

He gave her a curious look. "I have been off and on for quite a while."

"I've never seen you on any of the jobs before."

Logan shook his head as he started the truck. "I've been more off than on lately. I was here when they started on their first house."

She thought back and couldn't remember ever seeing him. "So was I."

"I helped lay the foundation and then helped on the roof."

"Oh." Now it made sense why she didn't see him. She'd come in after the foundation and then did a little bit of the interior work before she got too busy with school to come back.

He smiled. "The last house I worked on was finished about a month and a half ago. I had a lot of jobs for my business, so I wasn't able to get back into it until now." He chuckled as he turned on to the main road. "The Lord's ways sure are amazing, aren't they? You and I just met at your parents' house, and now we're working together here."

Amelia pursed her lips and glanced down. Yes, the Lord's ways were amazing, but she wasn't sure if it was the Lord or Logan ... or her mother who arranged this.

"Does Mama know where you were going?"

"I didn't tell her specifically where I'd be. I just said I had some things I needed to do, so I sent Brandon. Did you have a chance to meet him?"

"Yes." She clamped her mouth shut and looked out the window.

Logan chuckled.

She turned to him. "What's so funny?"

"Sometimes what you don't say is louder than what you do say."

"That makes no sense." She turned away from him again.

They rode in silence until they got to the kitchen renovation showroom. He turned off the ignition and stared at her until she looked directly at him. "Remember that the prices you see are higher than the price I pay as a contractor."

She nodded, got out, and started for the door. She didn't like the fact that she felt as though she'd been set up, but she had to admit he sure was nice.

"I wasn't finished telling you about the prices," he said as he put his hand on the door, blocking her from going inside.

She stopped and held her breath. What she hadn't counted on was the melty feeling she had in her tummy when he looked down at her.

"The owner here has agreed to donate the materials for the Christian Partnership project, as long as we stay in a certain price range. I'll show you the area we need to stay in for that."

"Okay." She lifted her eyebrow in what she hoped he saw as a challenge. "I take it he's a Christian?"

"Yes, he goes to my church." She was fully aware of the tightness of the muscles in his arm and the firmness of his jaw as he continued watching her.

She shifted and swallowed hard, finally breaking her gaze. "Anything else you need to tell me?"

Again, he laughed. "No, ma'am." He opened the door and made a grand sweeping gesture. "After you."

The moment she walked into the shop, she was

overcome with the vastness of the selection. She turned to Logan, and he laughed.

"It's a bit overwhelming, isn't it?"

She nodded. "Yes."

Without another word, he took her by the hand, led her to the far corner of the room, and stopped in front of the section with the countertop materials. "This is where we'll have to stay for the house we're building. After we pick something out, we have the rest of the store to look at for your parents' house." He paused and smiled. "Any thoughts?"

Amelia swallowed hard and nodded. "Okay, how about something light? The house is small, so I figured a lighter countertop would make the kitchen seem brighter and maybe a little bigger."

"I agree. At least that narrows it down somewhat."

They spent the next twenty minutes checking out all of the different light colored countertops, until Amelia finally settled on one she liked. "It has enough swirls for architectural interest but not so many to overwhelm the small kitchen."

"You sound like a designer." He inspected her selection and nodded. "And I agree that this is the best choice with the dark wood floors. It'll add some brightness that the kitchen needs. I'll get them to send out what we need as soon as possible." He motioned toward the rest of the store. "Now we need to pick several samples to take to your parents."

She grimaced. "This is where it gets difficult."

"Yes, I know, and that's why I didn't want to do it by myself. I don't know your mother very well, and you obviously do, so it's best for you to narrow it down."

"The kitchen on Magnolia Lane is huge, so we can go with any of them." Amelia thought for a moment as she pulled up a mental image of how the kitchen was now. "Did my mother say whether or not they're keeping the floors?"

"They are. Apparently, the tiles were imported, so they have to stay."

"Good," Amelia replied. "I've always thought those tiles were pretty and gave the place a homey feel."

He gave her an appreciative nod. "So that at least gives us a starting point. The countertops have to go well with the floor tiles."

As they discussed her parents' kitchen, Amelia realized how detailed Logan was and how he thought through every decision. That impressed her.

It took them another hour to select half a dozen choices to bring home for Mama to make the final decision. As they walked back to the truck, Logan placed his hand on the small of her back as though it was the most natural thing in the world. She stiffened at first, but as he walked her to the passenger door, she relaxed. Logan seemed like a good guy and one who sincerely cared about doing the right thing.

After they got back to the construction site, they parted ways. Logan brought the sample of what would be delivered later to the foreman, while Amelia went to help out with some of the final painting.

By the end of the day, she was exhausted. She hadn't forgotten about Logan, but she didn't expect to see him on her way to her car.

"Going home now?" he asked.

She nodded. As tired as she was, she was tempted to ask him to come over, but she decided not to.

"Let your mother know I appreciate her offer to have dinner with her and your dad, but this was too crazy of a day. I'll be there first thing Monday morning. If she doesn't like anything we picked, we can start over."

Amelia nodded. "I'll tell her."

All the way to Magnolia Lane, she thought about her day. As busy as she'd been, what stuck out most was the time she spent choosing countertops with Logan. She tried really hard, but she couldn't think of a bad thing about him.

"Nobody's that perfect." She laughed at the fact that she'd spoken those words aloud, even though she was the only person in the car.

This time, she pulled up behind the house and entered through the kitchen, where her mother sat at the table flipping the pages of a home decorating magazine. She glanced up and smiled as she looked at the box in Amelia's hands.

"What have you got there?"

Amelia put the box on the floor and pulled out some of the countertop samples. "I wasn't sure whether you preferred the look of granite or quartz, so I brought some of both. There are more in the car."

"I just read that quartz is less porous and more durable," her mother said. "But I like the patterns on the granite." She inspected the samples as Amelia placed them on the table.

"I'll be right back." Amelia went out to her car and got the rest of the samples. She brought them inside and placed them on the table. "Do any of these look good?"

Her mother nodded. "I actually like all of them." She glanced down at the floor. "Why don't we put all of them closer to the floor tiles and see which ones look best?"

"Remember that they won't be right up next to the floor tiles," Amelia reminded her. "The cabinets will be between them. Have you decided what to do about them yet?"

"I was torn between painting and staining. I've gone back and forth, but now I'm leaning toward paint. It gives me more options."

"By the way, did you know that Logan's involved with the same home-building ministry I am?"

Her mother grinned. "I found out when Brandon told me. I was hoping the two of you would see each other there."

"Mama." Amelia tilted her head forward.

"I know, I know. But you can't blame your mama for tryin' to help her baby find happiness."

That made Amelia laugh. Her mother would never see her as an adult who could make her own decisions, so she figured she might as well see the humor of it rather than get mad.

They chatted about the colors for a few more minutes before her mother said, "What does Logan think?"

"Huh?" Amelia cast a curious glance at her mother.

"Logan." Her mother pointed to the samples. "Which one does he like best?"

"Mama, it's really not up to him. He's not the one who'll have to live with it."

Her mother shrugged and looked away. "I'd still like to hear his thoughts."

"Oh, that reminds me. He said he'll be here first thing Monday morning."

"What time do you have to be at the school?" her mother asked.

"A little early. I have to redo the bulletin board and finish writing the test."

"Maybe you'll still be here when he arrives." Her

mother chuckled as she closed the magazine and walked toward the door. "I'm going to early services in the morning. Want to join me?"

Amelia shook her head. "I like the later services."

"What if I begged you to come with me?"

"I'd think you were plotting again." Amelia gave her a sideways glance. "Why?"

"Oh, nothing."

After her mother left the kitchen, she picked up all of the countertop samples and stacked them on the kitchen table. Then she got a drink of water before heading upstairs to her room.

*

Logan had remembered his thoughts about seeing Amelia—that if any part of his dream of working alongside her came true, he'd think about dating her. There was some irony here, and he doubted she'd get the humor. In fact, if he told her he had to ask her out because he'd dreamed about building a house with her, she'd probably assume he'd lost his mind. In fact, he was beginning to think that of himself.

Mrs. Sawyer had asked Logan to go to church with her in the morning. He worshiped at a different location of the same church, a satellite location closer to his house, but he told her that if he could get up early enough he'd meet her by the front of the building. He liked seeing the services live. The one close to his house had the same services on closed circuit TV.

Of course he realized what Mrs. Sawyer was doing. Her matchmaking skills weren't the best, and she wasn't the least bit subtle. He downed a glass of water and chuckled to himself. At least he didn't mind being around the other object of Mrs. Sawyer's matchmaking attempts. Amelia was awfully pretty, smart, and energetic. In fact, he appreciated people with motivation, and he couldn't think of anyone more driven than her.

However, he wondered why she stayed so busy. Granted, he was busy too, but she moved at a dizzying speed, never appearing to slow down. Everything she did as far as he could tell was for other people, completely the opposite of Jodi, the last girl he'd dated. He always had to work around her hair and nail appointments or shopping trips. Apparently, he was attracted to busy women. The difference with this one, though, was her selflessness in all she did.

After eating a sandwich over the kitchen sink, he washed the dishes and headed to bed. He picked up the men's devotional he'd been working his way through, read the next section, and then turned off the light. He must have fallen asleep immediately because he didn't remember anything after closing his eyes.

All the way to the church the next morning, he tried to imagine what he'd face in a few minutes. It was obviously important to Mrs. Sawyer for him to be there. He wondered if Amelia would be with her.

Chapter 4

He spotted Mrs. Sawyer standing on the church steps as he pulled into the parking lot. She stood alone but smiled and chatted with people as they entered the building. He was surprised by his disappointment at not seeing Amelia with her mom.

As soon as Mrs. Sawyer saw him coming toward her, she lit up. "Hey there, Logan. My husband is saving us a seat close to the front, so let's get on inside."

He followed her up the aisle and toward a pew where Mr. Sawyer sat looking as though he had no idea what his wife was up to. Now that Logan thought about it, he wondered how much Mrs. Sawyer had told her husband and if he even realized that his wife was matchmaking.

Mr. Sawyer stood and shook Logan's hand. "Good to see you, Logan. Melissa said you might join us."

"I'm happy to be here." Logan glanced up toward the front before turning back to the Sawyers. "It's always good to see the service live."

Mr. Sawyer shook his head. "I don't know why anyone would want to watch this on TV. It's always best when you have the pastor in the room with you."

His wife nudged him in the side. "That's not a nice thing to say."

"Just being honest."

The music started, so they all turned toward the front. Logan had to agree with Mr. Sawyer. It was so much better in person, especially sitting close to the front. When he'd come in the past, he typically arrived there in the nick of time, so he'd sat in the back.

After the services ended, he stood and stretched. "I guess I'd better be getting on home."

A panicked look came over Mrs. Sawyer's face. "Oh, no. You have to go to the Bible study. There's a special one for people your age."

Okay, now he understood. "Will Amelia be there?"

Her eyes darted around before she settled her gaze on him and smiled. "Maybe ... probably."

Logan couldn't help but laugh. Mrs. Sawyer wasn't good at hiding her intentions, but he thought that was very sweet. In fact, it was quite a nice compliment for her to like him enough to fix him up with her daughter.

"I don't want to intrude on her personal space."

Mrs. Sawyer lifted an eyebrow and gave him an odd look. "You're kidding, right?"

"If she doesn't expect me—"

"Look, Logan, she knows you attend church, and the Bible study has quite a few people attending. It's not exactly her personal space."

"Okay, point taken." He thought for a moment and tried to decide whether or not he should go. Besides, he really would like to see Amelia. Finally, he nodded. "Sure, I'll go. It's been a while since I've stuck around for the Bible study."

"So you might as well start now, right?" The look of pure joy on her face made his decision worthwhile.

"I hope it doesn't bother her if I'm there."

"Why should it bother her? This is a place of worship, not some private club."

He sighed. "You're right."

She gave him a big smile. "I generally am."

"Can you point the way? This place is so big, and I've never been to the Bible study on this campus."

She pointed to a hallway behind him. "Go all the way down that hall, turn left, and the classroom is right there. It's the biggest one in the building."

"Thanks, Mrs. Sawyer."

She laughed. "Have fun."

He gave a quick wave as he grinned back at her. "See you first thing tomorrow morning."

"Or you can come for dinner tonight, if you don't have any plans."

"Sorry, but I do have plans." As he headed toward the Bible study room, Logan thought about his plans. He'd promised Brandon to help him move a cabinet, and then they were going out for pizza. He'd much rather go to the Sawyers' house, but a promise was a promise, and he hated when people didn't honor their commitments.

He didn't have to worry about knowing where to go. As soon as he got to the long hallway, a long stream of twenty- and thirty-something people had lined up to go in. He looked around but didn't see Amelia. Maybe she decided not to come for the Bible study.

Logan had barely found a seat when he spotted her. She was deeply in conversation with some guy at the front of the room, and they seemed awfully comfortable around each other. A quick pang of jealousy shot through Logan, surprising him.

A woman sat down on his left. She gave him a shy look, glanced away, and giggled.

He cleared his throat and reached out to shake her hand. "Hi, I'm Logan Hawkins. And you are—?"

She shook his hand. "My name is Shay." She leaned back. "And this is my friend Jewel."

"It's nice to meet you, Shay and Jewel." He licked his lips and tried to think of something to say, but the guy Amelia had been talking to walked up to the podium and held up his hand to get everyone's attention. "Looks like the Bible study is about to start."

Both girls exchanged a glance and giggled. Logan

pulled out his phone, pulled up the Bible on his e-book app, found the scripture verse the man said they were studying, and turned his attention to the front. Throughout the Bible study, Logan did his best to pay attention to what the man was saying, but the fact that Amelia was right up there with him was distracting.

Logan kept trying to figure out what she was doing up there—if she was part of the program or if she was involved with the discussion leader. After they finished the Bible study, Amelia walked up to the podium, nodded to a couple of guys with guitars, and started signing. Goose bumps floated down his arms as he took in the angelic sound of her voice. Was there anything this woman couldn't do?

*

The second Logan walked into the room, Amelia felt that strange flush he caused any time they were together. She did her best to ignore him, but that was impossible.

Now, as she sang, she felt his penetrating gaze, so she looked everywhere but at him. She wondered what he was doing here.

After the song ended, she thanked everyone for coming and announced that refreshments were available in the back of the room. Everyone raced to the long row of tables with coffee, juice, pastries, and fruit ... everyone except Logan. He remained standing there, staring at her.

Their gazes locked, so there was no way she

could continue to pretend not to notice him. Her lips quivered into a shaky smile. He smiled back, giving her the sensation of the world falling off its axis.

The moment ended when he started walking toward her. "Hi, Logan. It's so nice to see you this morning. What brought you here?"

He shrugged. "I just thought it would be nice to see live church rather than a closed circuit sermon."

Amelia laughed. "I know what you mean. I always prefer to see the pastor and worship team in person." She shifted awkwardly from one foot to the other and tried to think of something to say. "I … um, are you planning to stay for church?"

An odd look flashed across his face before he nodded. "Yes, as a matter of fact, that's exactly what I'm planning to do."

She looked around for the girl who'd been sitting next to him in the Bible study before settling her gaze back on him. "Are you with someone?"

He shook his head. "No, I'm alone."

"Would you like to sit with me?" She held her breath as she watched his expression change to one she couldn't read.

"I would love to."

She heard a beeping sound coming from his pocket. "Oh, sorry, I forgot to silence my phone." He pulled his phone out of his pocket, read whatever was on the screen, and looked at her. "Looks like Brandon doesn't need me after all."

She gave him a curious look. "He doesn't need you for what?"

"Oh, I was supposed to go help him later this afternoon, and then we were going out for pizza. Apparently, some girl he's been talking to has invited him over for dinner, and he'd rather be with her." He chuckled. "Can't say I blame him."

"I like pizza." The instant those words escaped Amelia's mouth, her throat tightened. What on earth was she doing?

A surprised expression replaced his smile, and he nodded. "Then if you're not doing anything, why don't we go out for pizza this evening?"

"I didn't mean to ..." Amelia took a step back. An unfamiliar terror ripped through her. "I wasn't inviting—"

"I know you weren't, which was why I asked you." He tilted his head toward her. "Will you please go out for pizza with me tonight? I had my heart set on it, and if you don't go, I'll be forced to eat alone."

His comical expression made her laugh, in spite of her embarrassment. "Okay, since you put it that way, I'll go get pizza with you, but only under one condition."

"What's that?"

She didn't want this to seem too much like a date. "We split the bill."

"You don't have to—"

"That's the condition."

He held out both hands, palms up. "Then I guess

I have no choice but to agree."

"We'd better get to the sanctuary. Church will be starting soon."

Logan followed close behind her. "Where are we sitting?"

"I have a couple of favorite spots."

"It's completely up to you," he said. "I don't care where we sit, as long as I can hear your angelic voice during worship."

She stopped in her tracks. "My what?"

"Your voice," he said as he looked at her with admiration. "It's beautiful."

"Um ..." Now she was completely speechless. She'd been the one who led the singing at the end of every Bible study, but she didn't think anyone actually paid attention to her voice. Generally, as soon as she sang the first couple of words, everyone else joined in. Her face flamed as she met his gaze.

"Sorry if I embarrassed you."

Amelia gulped. "That's okay." She pointed to a pew close to the front. "How about there?"

Something registered on his face, but she couldn't tell what it was. She was about to suggest another pew, but he nodded. "Perfect."

Throughout the church service, he appeared to anticipate things before they happened. He even started smiling while the pastor was telling a story—but before the final funny comment was made. After the benediction, she stood and looked directly at him but didn't say anything.

He appeared uneasy. Finally, he said, "What? Do I have something on my face?"

She nodded. "Yes, you have a goofy expression on your face. What is going on with you, Logan?"

"What do you mean?"

"It's almost like you knew what the pastor was going to say before he even opened his mouth."

He gave her a sheepish look. "I have a confession to make."

"Okay, what did you do?"

"I accepted your mother's invitation to church this morning, so this was the second time I heard the sermon."

She nodded slowly. "I thought it was odd that you always seemed to know when the pastor was about to say something funny. Why didn't you tell me that earlier? I wouldn't have asked you to sit through it again."

"That's why I didn't tell you. I wanted to sit through it again ... with you."

Chapter 5

Logan felt bad about not saying anything, but once he got here, he really wanted to spend more time with Amelia. Now he didn't mess up any plans she might have made.

"Should I apologize?" he asked.

She cocked her head to one side. "Apologize? No, I'm actually glad you did this."

"Whew! That's a relief." He gestured toward the door. "Ready to go?"

As they walked out the door and through the parking lot, he wondered what to say next. She reached her car, stopped, and turned around to face him.

"So are we still on for pizza tonight?" she asked.

"Absolutely."

"Okay, where do you want to meet?"

"Your place. I'll pick you up."

"Okay. What time?"

"How about six? I like to eat early on Sunday nights, since I like to get an early start on Mondays."

"I'll see you at six." She unlocked her car before turning back to face him. "Oh, and by the way, I don't know about you, but I don't like to dress up for pizza."

"I wouldn't even consider dressing up for pizza."

She got in her car, waved, and drove away, leaving him standing there, staring after her. If someone had told him a week ago that he'd be dating the daughter of one of his clients, he wouldn't have believed it. He had a hard rule that business wouldn't ever cross the line into his personal life. But this was one of those times he couldn't help it. Amelia was just that adorable.

*

"Did you have a nice time in church today, sweetie?" Amelia's mother had her back to her as she put some sandwiches on a platter.

"It was okay."

"Just okay?"

Amelia laughed. "I'm kidding. I always like church. Now I have a question for you."

Her mother quickly put the remaining sandwiches on the platter. "Not now. I have to bring these out to your father on the patio. He's starving."

Amelia blocked her mother and folded her arms as she looked her in the eyes. "First, my question."

"Okay, but hurry."

"Why didn't you tell me you'd invited Logan to church?"

Her mother shrugged and let out a nervous giggle. "I didn't realize I had to ask your permission to invite a friend to church."

"That's not what I asked."

"I thought it would be nice to have him in church." Her mom lifted the platter. "If you'll please step aside, I'd like to bring your father his lunch."

Amelia did as she was told. As she watched her mother through the large picture window behind the breakfast nook, she thought about what her brother had said when he and his wife moved to Tennessee. Their mother had interfered enough times for him to be concerned about his marriage. Besides, he wasn't interested in the old house, nor did he want to stay in Biloxi. "Too humid and too many mosquitos," he'd said.

She stood there and watched her parents eating, talking, and laughing. It was nice to see that her parents' marriage seemed to be in good order. She knew they had one of those rare relationships that most people only dreamed of.

Most Sundays she spent at one of her ministries, but she needed to do some lesson planning and grading since school was coming to an end soon. She went to her room to work on it.

She was startled by the knock at her door. Her mother opened the door and smiled. "You didn't tell me you were going out with Logan tonight."

"Oh, sorry." Amelia rubbed her temples. "He'll be here in—" She glanced at the clock. "Oops. I lost track of time."

"Well, he's here now. I'll keep him entertained while you get ready." Before Amelia had a chance to respond, her mother left her room and closed the door behind her.

She'd already changed into jeans, so all she had to do was brush her hair and freshen her lipstick. She took one last glance in the full-length mirror before leaving her room.

The sensation she felt when she first spotted Logan made her stop in her tracks. It was a combination of freefalling and being in a tornado. She liked the feeling, but she didn't want him to notice.

His eyes sparkled as he grinned at her. "Your mom and I were just discussing the countertops. She wants to see more samples."

Sure she does. Amelia forced a smile. "One of us can stop by and pick up a few more—"

Her mother interrupted. "I was thinking that the two of you can go again."

The muscles in Amelia's cheeks burned for holding the smile so long. "Or better yet, why don't you go with him next time? That way you can see everything they have and get exactly what you want."

Her mother frowned. "Remember, I'm afraid I'd be way too overwhelmed with so many choices." Amelia knew her mother well enough to see through the act. "You know how I am."

"Yes, I do know how you are." Amelia turned to Logan and met his look of amusement. "Ready for some pizza?"

"Absolutely." He placed his hand on her back before turning toward her mother. "I won't keep her out too late. Tomorrow's a workday."

"That's okay. Stay out as long as you like. You're both adults."

As soon as they got in Logan's truck, Amelia let out a growl she'd been holding back. He laughed.

"Your mother means well," he said.

"Oh, I'm sure she does." Amelia didn't want to continue talking about her mother, so she changed the subject. "What's your next house project?"

"Something with Christian Partnership Ministries." He stopped for a light, turned, and grinned at her. "The guy I consider my spiritual father—the one who brought me to church for the first time—started it. I owe him my life."

"Oh. Are you talking about the infamous Joe Tatum?"

He gave a clipped nod as he accelerated after the light turned green. "The one and only. He's an amazing guy. Have you met him?"

"Once, but that was a couple of years ago." Amelia repositioned herself in her seat and turned to face him. "What's he like?"

"Pretty much what you see is what you get. He's no-nonsense, and he loves the Lord with all his heart."

"Why did he take you to church?" The instant Amelia asked, she cringed. She wasn't sure if she was opening a topic he didn't want to discuss.

The look on his face indicated otherwise. "My mom took off to 'find herself,' so it was just my dad and me. He worked a lot of hours, and when he was home, he was too busy to bother with church."

"Oh." She swallowed hard. "I'm sorry."

Logan shrugged. "That's okay. He eventually came around and accepted Christ before he passed away, and I'm happy to have someone like Joe in my life. He and his wife Molly were like second parents to me. They lived next door to us when I was growing up."

"Is Molly still living?"

"Oh yeah." Logan chuckled. "In fact, you've probably seen her at one of your missions. She's on the board of several, including the Interdenominational Food Bank."

Amelia thought for a moment before she remembered meeting someone named Molly. "I think I've seen her once too."

"Both of them are committed Christians who spend most of their resources on others, and that was how they got together when they were in high school. Joe once told me that when they found out they couldn't have children they didn't worry about it because all of the people they helped became their children ... including me. I think I was the most difficult one, though."

"How so?"

Logan's demeanor became more serious. "Let's just say that I went through a rebellious period in high school. I ran away a couple of times, and although my own dad didn't bother looking for me, Joe and Molly did. And they always found me." He pulled into the pizzeria parking lot and parked. "How about you? What was your childhood like ... other than golden?"

"What do you mean by golden?"

"You did grow up in a mansion, and your father is one of the business leaders in Biloxi."

She nodded, but something in his tone bugged her. "I didn't exactly rebel and run away, but I don't see my childhood as golden."

"Sorry. I was out of line." He opened his door. "Forget I ever said that."

For the remainder of their time together, that was all Amelia could think about. How could she help it if she was raised in a family that had money? She had a nice time, but it would have been better if he hadn't made those comments.

Her mother was waiting up when she got home, an expectant look on her face as she pounced on Amelia with questions. "Did y'all have a good time? How was he? Did he ask you out again?"

Amelia held up both hands. "Yes we had a good time, he was nice, and no he didn't ask me out again."

Her mother's expression fell. "I was hoping ..." She flipped her hand from the wrist. "Oh, never mind. You'll see him again. It'll take him weeks—

maybe even months—to finish the work on this old place."

This old place was one of the nicest homes in Biloxi, and her parents were having it renovated simply because they were tired of it—not because it needed anything. She thought about some of the people who were grateful for the small houses she helped build.

Now that she thought about it, she could see why Logan made the comments he did. He must think she was a spoiled brat who got everything she wanted. How was he to know that she didn't want much ... at least not for herself?

"Amelia?"

She glanced up at her mother. "Yes?"

"Have you been listening to me? I feel as though I've been sitting here talking to myself for the last several minutes."

"I'm just tired." Amelia turned toward her room. "I'll see you in the morning. Don't expect me to wait around for Logan. I have to be at the school early." Before her mother had a chance to say another word, she left and went straight to her room.

*

Logan could have kicked himself a dozen times after speaking his mind before they even went into the pizza place. He thought about all the time Amelia committed to helping others. He was way out of line.

He actually liked Amelia, although he couldn't

imagine two people with such different backgrounds getting together romantically. As soon as that thought entered his mind, he realized he was already romantically involved with her in his mind.

The small house he'd paid cash for last year was so small that four of them could fit into the Sawyer mansion and still have room left over. But it was his, and he could do whatever he wanted to with it … at least he could when he had time. The problem was when he finished work and helping with the Christian Partnership Ministries, he had very little time for himself. This house had pretty much become a place to eat, sleep, and hang his belongings.

Sundays were always his lightest day of the week, but most of the time he had thoughts of a busy Monday hanging over him. However, today he didn't think about anything beyond the moment. Amelia Sawyer had that effect on him. He wanted to be with her as much as possible, but he felt his old surly self bubble to the surface every once in a while.

He squeezed his eyes shut and prayed for wisdom. Amelia couldn't help the fact that she grew up in a home that was as close to perfect as he'd ever seen, while his upbringing was the opposite.

Chapter 6

Amelia wasn't about to stick around the house any longer than necessary on Monday morning. She knew her mother hoped Logan would arrive before she left, but she didn't think it would be a good way to start the week. She needed to concentrate on the kids in her class since the school year was coming to an end soon.

She checked her mailbox in the back of the school office and turned around to face one of the assistant principals. He was a nice looking man, just a few years older, and he was clearly attracted to her. She gave him a shaky smile and tried to sidestep him, but he continued to block her.

"I need to go to my classroom."

He smiled and nodded. "I'm still trying to figure out if you're not interested or just playing hard to get."

Amelia surveyed the situation by looking around

and then back at him. It was time to take the biggest risk she'd ever taken in her three-year teaching career. "I like you, Paul, but as a boss." She held his gaze and squared her shoulders. "Nothing else."

He tightened his lips in resignation, offered a clipped nod, and stepped aside. "I understand. I'm sorry if I bothered you."

She felt bad for him. Paul Morrison was a sweet man who, although he'd come close a few times, had never completely crossed the line, so she never doubted his sincerity. Now she wished she'd leveled with him sooner.

"You haven't bothered me. I'm sorry that I might have given you the impression—"

He held up a hand. "No need to apologize. You haven't done anything wrong." He extended a hand. "Friends?"

She accepted his handshake and nodded. "Friends."

"If there is anything I can do to assist with the testing, let me know, okay?"

"Will do."

After Amelia left for her classroom, she felt as though a humongous load had lifted from her shoulders. Now she wouldn't have to dread seeing Paul in the office anymore ... at least that was what she hoped. It might be a little awkward for a while, but the time away during the summer would take care of that.

The morning went well, but it still seemed to

drag. She managed to do everything on her list, but images of Logan kept popping into her mind at the most unexpected of times. During lunch, Dawn, one of the other teachers commented on the new house going up a couple of blocks from where she lived.

"Is your group the one building it?" she asked.

Amelia nodded. "That's the one I've been working on."

"I've never seen so many people on one construction site. Are they all from your church?"

"No, it's an organization that involves several churches in Biloxi."

Dawn glanced down at the table and looked up at Amelia, smiling. "My husband and I have talked about going to church. Until we saw what your group was doing with that house, we didn't see it being that important."

Amelia understood what the other teacher was saying—that she'd never seen practical application of the gospel. She nodded. "We realize what we're doing won't earn us a spot in heaven, but we feel like it's giving a family a boost with what they need most—a safe and secure place to raise their family."

"I like that." A pensive look came over Dawn. "I'll tell my husband that we need to check it out. He's quite handy with a hammer, so maybe we can help with the house … that is, if it's not to late."

"It's never too late. After we finish that house, we'll be looking for another family to help."

"Good. Now all we have to do is find a church to attend. Tell me more about yours."

Amelia was happy to talk about where she went to church and some of the programs they offered. Dawn had a couple of children—one in elementary and the other in high school. She seemed pleased to know that there were programs for both of them.

Finally, Amelia stood up and carried her wrappers to the trashcan. "Better get back to my room. See you tomorrow."

She was tired and happy when the workday ended. Now all she had to do was go home, change into some jeans, and head over to the construction site. It looked like they might only be there a few more days, and hopefully by the end of the week they'd have the place inspected and ready to turn over to the family.

Fortunately, when she got to Magnolia Lane, no one was home, so she didn't have to answer any questions. It took her ten minutes to get out of her school clothes and into something more rugged.

When she arrived at the construction site, she spotted Logan right away. His face was flaming red, and he appeared extremely frustrated. As soon as she parked her car, she hopped out and ran toward him.

"What's going on?" she asked.

His eyes widened, and he shook his head. "Go take a look at the countertops."

He followed her inside. The instant she entered

the kitchen, she saw the problem. "Why did you change the countertops?"

"I didn't. That's the problem."

"They are pretty, but they don't exactly go with the house."

"I know. And they cost nearly twice as much as the ones we were supposed to get."

"Who has to pay?" Amelia asked. "I know they're out of the price range of what the store was donating."

"That's just it. The people who delivered the materials don't have any idea."

"Can't you just call the guy at the store?"

"Better yet, I'm going there, and I'd like for you to join me, in case we have to pick something else, since they might not have our first choice in stock."

"I—" She glanced around looking for something she needed to do onsite. But everything appeared to be getting done. "Okay."

As soon as they arrived at the store, the salesman approached. "How do you like the upgrade?"

Amelia and Logan exchanged a glance before Logan turned back to the salesman. "We didn't ask for an upgrade."

"I know, but some woman by the name of Melissa Sawyer did."

"That's my mom."

"I thought so," the salesman said. "When she came in, she said she won't settle for anything but the best of everything for her daughter." He puffed up his chest, clearly pleased with himself. "And when she said she'd cover the difference, I showed her what we had."

Amelia made a face. Logan, on the other hand, let his feelings out. "You should have checked with me first. We can't accept those countertops."

Now the salesman looked like someone had punched him. "Why not? They're very nice countertops." He paused. "The very best we carry."

"They don't go with the house."

Logan and the salesman had a stare-down that lasted long enough to make Amelia squirm. Finally, she spoke up. "I agree with Logan."

The salesman slowly shook his head and took a step back. "I'll have to talk to the boss about this. We thought you'd be happy."

"I'm not happy about this in the least. We're supposed to turn the keys over to the homeowners in less than a week, so we expect this to be fixed immediately."

"I don't know—"

Amelia saw the guy's distress, so she leaned toward Logan and whispered, "Maybe we can talk to the homeowners and push it back by a few days." She felt terrible that her mother's good intentions had caused this problem.

He adamantly shook his head. "We need to honor our commitment to the family." He paused. "I'll cover the expense."

The salesman excused himself to go call the owner of the shop, while Logan walked over to the countertop materials to look around. She felt terrible for the salesman who'd been caught in the middle.

A half hour later, they had the problem resolved. The salesman said the owner agreed to do a rush delivery later that day, and he'd personally see to it that everything was how they wanted it. In exchange, Logan agreed to take the countertop for a discount and make it work for his house. But he still seemed upset.

*

Although Logan was upset that Mrs. Sawyer did what she did, he realized she thought she was doing something good. He really needed to talk to her, but had no idea what to say.

Logan knew he wasn't acting all that friendly on the way back to the site, but he had a lot to process in his mind. She kept casting curious glances his way during the drive back to the construction site, but he forced himself to look straight ahead and not give in, no matter what.

The biggest problem in his mind was how this incident reminded him of the social differences between him and Amelia. She grew up in a big home with loving parents, while he had to make his way in the world, and if something bad happened, he had to deal with it. No one would be there to catch him, and he certainly couldn't go running to someone if he had a flood in his house.

Once he pulled into the parking lot, she got out, gave him a brief look, and then ran off toward the house. He sat in the truck and watched her stop and talk to a couple of people working on the landscaping. After she went inside, he got out of his truck and went looking for the foreman.

He finally found Andrew in the main bathroom. Andrew glanced up and waved but continued chatting with the plumber.

"Can I see you for a sec?" Logan asked.

"Sure, I'll be right there." Andrew finished his conversation with the plumber before stepping out into the hallway. "This place is just about ready to be turned over, but the countertop ..." He made a face.

"That's what I wanted to talk to you about." Logan explained what had happened, leaving out the part about his feelings. "I'm sure Mrs. Sawyer meant well, but she clearly didn't realize what all it impacted."

Andrew chewed on his bottom lip and rubbed the back of his neck. "I sure hope they come soon. We can't wait around too much longer before adding the backsplash."

As soon as he said that, one of the landscapers came in. "There's some guy from that kitchen design place who says he's here to change out the countertops."

Logan glanced at Andrew. "The salesman said they'd try to make it today, but I have to admit I didn't expect it to happen this quickly."

It took about an hour to get the more expensive counter off and the new one on. Logan had already paid for the one they were removing, so he instructed the guys to follow him home. It was already dark, so there weren't many people left at the site. Amelia had obviously left for the day. At least he didn't have to face her on the way to his truck.

Chapter 7

Amelia walked into the house on Magnolia Lane and headed straight for her room, only to be cut off by her mother. She tried to walk around her, but she couldn't.

"You don't think you can just walk in here this late and get away with not saying something, do you?" her mother asked.

"I ..." Amelia sighed. She wasn't in the mood to argue, which she knew they would do if she brought up her mother's interference. "I'm exhausted. It's been a long day."

"Then talk to me about it. I want to hear all about how your day went. Did you see Logan?"

Amelia knew that was the whole point of her interception, so she nodded. "Yes, in fact, that's why I'm home so late."

Her mother smiled. "I'll take that as a good sign."

Now there was no way Amelia could keep quiet. "No, it's totally not a good sign. We spent way too much time fixing a problem that someone else created."

"Someone else is interfering in yours and Logan's relationship? Who on earth would want to do that?"

"Mama, you really shouldn't have gotten involved with the house we're working on.

A horrified look came over her mother. " I didn't do anything wrong."

"Tell you what. Let me put my purse away and get into my pajamas. We can talk in the kitchen."

"Okay, but don't take too long. I'm dying to know what I did that has you so worked up."

"I'm not worked up," Amelia countered.

"Oh yes you are. I can see it on your face. You've never been able to hide your feelings from me." Her mother lingered for a few seconds, concern etched on her face.

When Amelia finally managed to escape to her room, she tossed her purse on the dresser and flopped over on her bed. This was one of the biggest reasons she preferred being on her own. Her apartment was small and not nearly as luxurious as her family home, but it was hers, and she enjoyed the peace and quiet.

Amelia had never been one to think that the opulence she'd grown up with was necessary. In fact, she liked a simpler lifestyle without so many extras that overshadowed what was really important. Although she never doubted her mother's faith in God, she often saw that He took a backseat to so many insignificant things. She not only lived in this gorgeous mansion, she wore nothing but designer clothes. When she found out that Amelia did some thrift shopping, she acted as though Amelia was doing something terribly wrong.

"But why?" she'd asked. "You can have anything you want. All you have to do is ask."

That was exactly what Amelia didn't want. She enjoyed the thrill of the hunt. In fact, the only designer clothes she liked to wear were those she paid less than half of their original cost. It wasn't just about the money. It was more about keeping things simple and lower maintenance.

After she changed into her pajamas, she picked up her phone and saw that she'd missed a message. It was from the manager of her apartment complex, letting her know that they'd repaired all of the damage and cleaned it up. Now it was ready for her to move back in. Oh, and she'd get a free month for her trouble. That made her smile, until she remembered that she'd have to break the news to her mother.

Her mother sat at the kitchen table with a pot of tea and two cups. "Have a seat, Amelia. Sounds like we might be here a while."

"I can't stay up too late. Remember, I have school tomorrow."

"Yes, of course. But we do have some things to

talk about, obviously."

Amelia sat down as her mother poured her a cup of tea she probably wouldn't drink. She stared at the cup before looking up at her mother.

"What did I do ... or say that you think was interfering?"

"Mama ... I, uh—" Amelia clamped her mouth shut and swallowed hard.

"Go on. Don't hold back."

"Why did you go to the kitchen place and swap out the countertops that Logan and I chose for the Christian Partnership house?"

"Oh, that." Her mother waved her hand around. "I was there looking at the selection—and you were right. They have a lot of beautiful materials."

"Back to the house we're building," Amelia reminded her. "We'd already picked what we wanted."

"But that was in their economy selection. Wouldn't it be nice to present the family with the best that money can buy?"

"Only if that's what's best for them." Amelia pondered how to say what needed to be said in a way that wouldn't make her mother defensive, but that seemed impossible.

"Don't you like what I picked? It's really nice."

"Yes, I agree. It's really nice, but it doesn't match the rest of the kitchen. It overpowers it."

Her mother's chin quivered. "What can I do to make things better?"

"Logan and I already straightened it out, so you

don't have to do anything."

"Then everything is all better?" Her mom's eyes lit up, as she looked Amelia directly in the eyes.

"Yes, everything is all better." At least, with the countertop it was *all better*. Amelia still hadn't figured out what had made Logan become so quiet.

"You don't sound happy about something."

Amelia briefly considered telling her mother about Logan's instant change of mood and decided against it. "It's just been a crazy busy day. I really need to get some rest."

"I hope you don't plan to do any of your charity work tomorrow, sweetie. You need your rest. I'd hate to see you collapse from exhaustion."

"Please don't do this, Mama. We're handing the keys over to the family in just a few days. I have to go work at the house."

Her mother shook her head in disapproval. "I don't like what you're doing a bit. You know that God doesn't measure your exhaustion and give you extra points for working your fingers to the bone, don't you?"

"Yes, of course. But this is something I feel led to do." She held her mother's scrutinizing gaze. "Something I really want to do. I like it. It brings me pleasure."

"I reckon I can't stop you. You're an adult and can come and go as you please, although you are living under our roof."

Mother had just given her the perfect opening. "By the way, I got a text message about the apartment. It's ready for me to move back in."

Her mother placed her hand on Amelia's. "You don't have to move back out, sweetie. In fact, I don't even know why you'd want to do that when you have such a lovely home here."

Forcing a smile, Amelia nodded. "Yes, it is a ... lovely home. But I like being on my own." She stood and stretched. "I really need to go to bed now. G'night, Mama."

She left her mother sitting in the kitchen alone, probably wondering what she could say to convince Amelia to stay in the house on Magnolia Lane. Nothing would keep Amelia from going back to her apartment—especially now. Her desire for independence had been validated by her mother's interference, as well meaning as it was.

She hadn't taken a single day off from school the entire year, so she asked for a personal day. Finding a substitute this time of year wasn't easy, but she finally found someone who could fill in for her on the following Monday. She spent the remainder of the week helping finish the ministry house after she got off work. Logan was there when she arrived each afternoon, but he was as focused on the work as she was.

On Friday night, the family arrived at the house, all of them wearing huge smiles. The mom, dad, and each of the children cut a section of the ribbon at the front door, while all of the workers looked on and applauded. By the time they walked inside and saw how wonderful their new home was, there wasn't a dry eye in the crowd. This was the best reward Amelia could think of for all of the hard work she and dozens of other people had put into this place.

"Looks like it was a success after all."

The sound of Logan's voice so close behind her caused her to spin around. She looked up into his eyes and almost fell over backward. If she thought she was attracted to him before, but now that she hadn't spoken to him in several days, she realized it was more than a basic attraction that would fade away. Her heart thudded, and her mouth went dry. She opened her mouth but couldn't speak. So she just nodded.

The family who'd taken possession of the house stood on the front porch and looked out over the workers. "We appreciate this more than you'll ever know. Y'all have exemplified the love of Christ by giving so much of your time and your money." The husband cleared his throat before continuing. "If you're ever in the neighborhood, please feel free to stop by for a cup of coffee."

Logan glanced down at Amelia and smiled. "They really are a sweet family."

"I'm glad we can help people who have fallen on hard times."

His expression tightened. "Yes, a lot of people will never understand what it's really like to fall on hard times."

She studied his staid expression and didn't know what to say. He clearly had a lot going on—and if he ever wanted her to know what it was, he'd tell her.

The ceremony for the family lasted another fifteen minutes. Finally, Andrew went up to the porch with the family, asked all the people to bow their heads, and said a prayer. After the last *Amen*, people scattered. Some walked down to the café around the corner, while others went to their cars. Amelia was in the latter group because she wanted to get her things ready to move back into her apartment.

Her mother greeted her in the driveway. "I put a plate of dinner in the fridge. You can heat it up in the microwave."

"Are you going somewhere?"

Her mother nodded. "Your daddy wants to see a movie. We won't be gone long."

Amelia was surprised her parents would go somewhere the last night she was in the house, but it was actually a blessing for her. She'd dreaded her mother's pleas to reconsider and her dad's silence that let her know he wasn't happy about the situation.

After eating dinner, she went up to her room and started packing. Some of her things were still in boxes, so she lined them up along the wall. Then she went outside to enjoy one of the things she knew she'd miss about Magnolia Lane—the aromatic flowers that lingered on the trees along the driveway. They always smelled sweetest at this time of day.

She closed her eyes, inhaled deeply, and then slowly let it out. When she opened her eyes, she saw Logan's truck coming toward the house.

Chapter 8

He parked in the circular driveway out front and got out. "I'm here to see your mother."

"She's not home," Amelia said, doing everything she could to keep her voice steady. "She and Daddy went to see a movie."

"That's odd. She called me about an hour and a half ago, saying she needed for me to stop by the house tonight."

Amelia groaned. Even when she wasn't here, Mama had her hand in other people's business.

Logan chuckled. "Looks like we've been set up." He glanced around.

"We sure have." Her gaze locked with his, and she couldn't help but smile. There was an attraction she couldn't deny … and a connection simply based on the fact that they were on the same side in her mother's frustrating scheme.

He smiled back and let out a soft chuckle, as

though he'd just heard a private joke. "You know, this place is really pretty this time of day."

"I agree. I love magnolias."

"Apparently whoever planted these trees did too. There are quite a few of them." He inhaled deeply. "And they sure do smell good."

"That's why I came out here … you know, to smell the magnolias." She paused and studied him. "If you like them so much, why don't you plant some in your yard?"

"Maybe one of these days. I haven't even had time to renovate the inside." He gave her one of his side grins that nearly took her breath away. "I'm so busy renovating other people's houses."

"It's good that you're busy, though, right?"

"Yes, of course." He pointed to the house. "Why don't we go sit on the porch?"

Without saying a word, she turned around and walked toward the house. She could hear him walking behind her.

"This house is a classic," he continued once they found their places—her on the porch swing and him on a rocking chair. "From the thick white columns out here to the intricately carved detail in all of the chair railing and crown molding inside, you can tell that someone paid quite a bit of attention to detail."

"I've heard that my great-grandfather was a real taskmaster when it came to having everything just so." Amelia enjoyed the gentle sway of the swing and the air tinged with the sweetness of the magnolias as she chatted with Logan. She loved sharing such a peaceful moment with him.

"I'm not surprised," Logan said. "There are quite a few extras inside that let me know he probably oversaw the construction, and it doesn't appear that it was all for his convenience. The built-in flour bin in the kitchen probably helped whoever cooked."

Amelia nodded. "Mama hates that flour bin, so that's where she stores her dish towels."

"Back in the day, women used to mix their biscuit dough right in the flour bin. They'd make a well in the center of the flour, pour in the ingredients, and knead it until they had a ball of dough. Then they'd pick it up and plop it onto a floured countertop where they rolled it out."

She tipped her head to the side. "How do you know so much about making biscuits the old fashioned way?"

"I majored in history in college."

That was the first she'd ever heard of that. "What made you go from history to renovating houses?"

"After I graduated from college, I taught for a couple of years. I did a little bit of home remodeling on the side."

"I had no idea you were a teacher. Why did you stop? Didn't you like it?"

"I liked it okay, but the remodeling and renovation business really took off. I had to make a decision, so I chose working on houses. I've always liked working with my hands." He rocked back and forth while holding her gaze. "At least I specialize in older homes, so my history degree isn't going to waste."

"True." It was strange how Logan's revelation gave her a different view of him. She never would have imagined him as a teacher, but now that she knew he was, she could see it.

"Where did you teach?"

"Gulfport High School."

"Interesting." She turned toward the yard and inhaled the fragrant air once again. "High school is a challenge."

"Talking about a challenge, I also taught driver's ed."

Amelia laughed. "Now that definitely is a challenge. It's good that you lived to tell about it."

He lifted an eyebrow in a comical way. "There were times I wondered."

"Oh, I'm sure." Amelia couldn't help but smile again as she held his gaze. When he smiled back, she felt as though someone had pushed her swing into the clouds. Something shifted between them at that moment, and she could tell that he noticed it too.

"Will I see you again after you go back to your apartment?" he asked softly.

She pulled her lips between her teeth and nodded. "Yes … that is, if you want to."

"I do." He stopped rocking and leaned forward, placing his elbows on his knees but not once taking his gaze off hers. "In fact, I'd like to help you move ... that is, if you need help."

She'd planned to make the move herself by taking her things over in several trips. Having his assistance would make it so much easier in some ways, but if he kept looking at her like this, in other ways, it would be more difficult.

"Well?" he asked. "Since you aren't answering, I'll assume implied consent. What time would you like me here in the morning?"

Amelia smiled at his choice of words. "Implied consent, huh? Sounds like a history teacher term."

"It's more of a salesman's term. So how about it? Have I sold you on my services?"

"What's the cost?" She glanced away, and then turned back to him, her head tilted.

"How about dinner?"

She nodded. "That's fine, but you might have to wait a few days so I can pick up a few things at the grocery store."

"Okay. In that case, I'll take you to dinner tomorrow night."

"Is that implied consent?"

"No, that's more like begging. I can't believe I'm saying this, Amelia, but I would like to spend more time with you, and that's the best thing I can come up with now."

"Why can't you believe it?"

He slowly shook his head. "Every once in a while some well meaning woman decides to set me up with her daughter. And that has never worked out for me. Until now." He stood and smoothed the front of his jeans. "I know you have a lot to do tonight, so I should probably leave."

She wanted more than anything to invite him in and talk some more, but he was right. She had quite a few things to do to get ready to move back into her apartment. And she needed some time to think.

"Do you have to get your key, or does your old one still work?" he asked.

"As far as I know, my old one still works, but I'll find out for sure in the morning." She followed him across the porch, down the steps, and toward his truck, where they stopped and turned to face each other.

He started to turn toward his truck but stopped. "What time do you want me here?"

"What time can you be here?"

"Whenever you want me here." The look in his eyes pulled her in. She took a tentative step toward him, and before she realized what was happening, he reached for her hand and pulled her closer. "Unless you protest in the next two seconds, I'm going to kiss you."

Chapter 9

"No protests here."

Logan thought about his decision to resist his desire to be with Amelia, but the pull toward her was too strong. Her combination of strength and vulnerability overpowered everything that concerned him, and all he wanted was to hold her. They might have come from different backgrounds, but what he saw was a strong, compassionate, beautiful woman who had the ability to own his heart.

She gave him a curious look, and that undid his resolve even more. Without another thought, he wrapped one arm around her waist and placed the other hand behind her head as he planted his lips on hers. The long, lingering kiss mixed with the fragrance around them provided a blend of sensations that would forever linger in Logan's mind.

After he pulled away, he took another look at Amelia. She offered a shy smile and then glanced down at the ground. He'd never seen her behave this way before, and the very thought that he had anything to do with it gave him an odd sense of joy.

"What time should I be here in the morning?" he repeated.

"Is 9:00 too early?"

He shook his head. "If you asked me to be here before the sun comes up, I'd do it."

She grinned. "I won't do that to you ... or to myself. I'll see you around nine."

It took every bit of will power to not grab her and give her another kiss. He backed away a couple of steps before he finally turned and got in his truck. As he pulled away and drove down the long, magnolia-lined driveway, he glanced in his rearview mirror and saw her standing in front of the house watching.

He couldn't help but smile all the way home. If one kiss from Amelia could do that to him, he knew he wanted more.

However, once he walked into his house, the old doubts began to creep back into his head. He liked Amelia, and after that kiss, there was no doubt in his mind that she liked him. But that didn't negate the fact that she'd been born into a lifestyle he'd never enjoyed. If he opened his heart to her, he risked experiencing pain he'd avoided ever since his mother left.

He wasn't sure if he could deal with that again.

The first time was unavoidable, but now he had some control. The risk was great, but would it be worse if he didn't take a chance? The more he thought about it the more he realized what a huge mistake he'd make if he opened his heart to her too quickly.

*

Amelia couldn't remember ever feeling so giddy. She liked Logan more than she ever dreamed she would. He'd acted a little bit moody a couple of times, but he was a busy man. Besides, she couldn't honestly say she'd never been testy.

That kiss—that perfect kiss—left her floating a few inches off the ground. Once she got inside the house after he left, she was happy no one else was there. She didn't feel like explaining the goofy smile she couldn't wipe off her lips.

Her mother would be pleased, but Amelia didn't want to admit anything ... at least not yet. But if she and Logan continued on this trajectory, she'd concede that her mother had been right all along when she started matchmaking. From what she could tell, they were perfect for each other. They had common interests, they were both Christians, and that kiss ... well, that kiss was one she'd forever hold in her memory.

She went to her room and finished getting ready for the move back to her apartment. Then she stacked the boxes outside her bedroom door. Her parents still weren't home, so she decided to leave them a note letting them know what time she'd be moving out before she went to bed.

That night she had the best sleep she'd had in a while. She woke up feeling better than she had since her apartment flooded.

She showered and got dressed before heading down to the kitchen where her mother stood in front of the stove cooking eggs. Her mother grinned at her and pointed to the coffee pot.

"Pour yourself a cup of coffee. The eggs will be ready in just a few minutes."

"Thanks, Mama. You didn't have to go to all this trouble."

"It's your last morning here …" Her mother glanced over her shoulder and smiled. "I want it to be a good one."

"Thanks."

"So how did you do last night?" Mama scooped some eggs onto a plate and carried them over to the table. "Did you get everything packed?"

Amelia nodded. "I did." The look her mother gave her was humorous and filled with questions. "Why?"

"Just wondering." She went to the stove and put more eggs on a plate. "Your father left early this morning to interview a new manager for one of the stores. I thought it would be a good time for us to have … you know … a mother-daughter chat."

"Sounds good." Amelia shoved a forkful of eggs into her mouth and looked at her mother. After she swallowed, she asked, "What do you want to chat about?"

"I don't know. I guess I just wondered how things were for you. Did anything interesting happen last night while your dad and I were at the movies?"

"Well, yes, sort of." Amelia grinned at her mother whose eyebrows shot up with anticipation. "I found a few things I'd been looking for."

"Like what?"

"My collection of Mac lipsticks."

"Is that all?"

"What do you mean *is that all*? I've been looking for my favorite tube of lipstick since I've been here." It took every bit of self-restraint Amelia had not to laugh at her mother's eagerness. And it was so much fun to tease her. "Oh, I also found those denim cutoffs. They'd fallen to the floor of the closet, and my suitcase was on top of them."

"Oh." Her mother wrapped her hands around her coffee mug as she looked down at the table.

Amelia couldn't keep doing this to her, so she finally blurted, "By the way, Logan showed up."

"That's a relief ... er, I mean that's nice. So how did it go?"

Her lips instantly tingled at the memory of the kiss, but she wasn't about to give her mother that much satisfaction. "It went well. He said you asked him to come."

An instant look of distress flashed over her mother's face. "I just said—"

Amelia held up a hand. "Don't worry about it. I'm fine about seeing him. In fact, he's coming at

9:00 to help me move back to my apartment. So instead of taking three trips, it'll only take one since he has a truck."

"I can't say I'm happy about having you move out, but at least you have Logan."

"I don't exactly *have* Logan. He's just helping me move."

"You know what I mean, Amelia." Her mother never looked away as she took a sip of her coffee. "And you have to admit that there is something pretty special about Logan."

Amelia nodded. "He's a nice guy, and he seems to want to help people." She grinned as she carried her plate and mug to the sink. "I'm happy that he has chosen to help me move. It sure will make things go more quickly."

Her mother shook her head and made a face. "I give up. Let me know if there's anything I can do to help."

"Will do." With that, Amelia left for her room.

She'd already done most of the work, so all she had left was to strip the bed and carry the sheets to the laundry room. Her parents' housekeeper would be here a little later, and she'd learned the hard way that Sylvia didn't like anyone else messing with her duties. So Amelia placed the sheets in the basket beside the washer.

As soon as the doorbell rang at precisely 9:00, Amelia flung it open, expecting to see a very happy looking Logan who was eager to get started. Instead, she stood before a man with his hands in his pockets, looking like he hadn't slept in days.

"Got your stuff ready to go?" he asked.

"I do." She tilted her head, narrowed her eyes, and looked at him quizzically. "What's wrong, Logan? Did something happen?"

He shook his head. "No, nothing happened. Where is your stuff?"

She pointed toward the stairs. "I've got everything in boxes outside my bedroom door."

He let out an odd grunting sound before turning and heading up the stairs. "Let's get this done, okay?"

She sucked in a breath and slowly let it out. "Okay. I'll put the suitcases in my car."

It took them about thirty minutes to load up her car and his truck. "I'll follow you," he said. "But I know where the apartment complex is, so don't worry about losing me if I'm not right behind you."

"Okay." Her mother had left for the morning, so all she had to do was go back in and get her purse.

She'd come back sometime tomorrow to thank her parents and bring them a gift. One thing her mother always stressed was the importance of proper etiquette when being a guest in someone's home. Even though her parents disagreed, she considered herself a guest when she stayed with them.

As soon as she got out, she told Logan she needed to check in and let the manager know she was moving back. He nodded and leaned against her car. "I'll wait right here."

They'd already changed the locks, so the manager handed her a new key. "New carpet, fresh paint, new furniture, and a new washing machine. You're essentially getting a brand new place."

Logan barely glanced up when she returned. "Ready to get his over with?" he said.

She nodded, still confused by his strange behavior. All she could think about last night was his kiss, and she'd hoped to repeat it today. But from the looks of things, that wouldn't happen again any time soon."

The two of them went back and forth between the parking lot and the apartment, placing things according to the labels on the boxes. When they had the last box in the apartment, Logan walked over to the door of his truck.

"I guess I'll be seeing you around. Have fun putting all of your stuff away."

His demeanor was distressing. "But what about dinner?"

He sighed. "I told you I'd take you to dinner, so I will. What time do you want me to pick you up?"

Amelia blinked. She felt like crying, but she bit her lip to relocate the pain from her heart.

He offered a hint of a smile, waved, and started to get into his truck. She couldn't let him go like that.

"Logan, wait." She ran toward the truck.

He stopped and turned toward her. "What? Did we forget something?"

She nodded. "Come here, please."

"Where?"

"Right here." She pointed to the ground in front of her.

"Why? What do you need?"

"Please stop asking questions. I just want you to come here."

He hesitated for a split second before doing as she asked. As soon as he stopped, she grabbed him by the collar and pulled his face toward hers. She stood on her tiptoes and kissed him on the lips. At first, she thought he might relax and enjoy the moment, but he didn't. Instead, he pulled away, rubbed the back of his neck, and headed for his truck again.

"Logan?"

He shook his head. "I really need to go now. I'm helping lay the foundation for the next Christian Partnership house."

She was so confused she didn't know what to do or say. "Do you want to forget about dinner?"

"Why?" he asked. "Do you?"

"I ... I don't know."

"Let me know when you decide." Without another word, he got in his truck.

Amelia stood and watched as he pulled out of the parking lot without another word. She had no idea what had just happened, and she was devastated.

She spent the remainder of the day unpacking and putting everything away. By the time she got to the box filled with decorations, though, she ran out of steam. Her earlier jubilant mood had been replaced by disappointment like none she'd ever experienced.

When her phone rang, a brief moment of hope rushed through her. But when she looked on her caller ID, the disappointment returned. It was her mother.

"Hey, Mama. What's up?"

"I saw that your room has been cleaned out. How are you and Logan doing with the unpacking?"

"Logan isn't here, but I'm pretty much done. All I have to do is hang a few pictures and find spots for some knickknacks."

"Where is Logan?"

Amelia sighed. "He left to go help lay the foundation for the next Christian Partnership house."

"Why didn't you go with him?"

"I have to get my house in order."

"Yes, of course. But I thought the two of you … well, I thought maybe—"

"You might want to start thinking about something else."

"Amelia!"

"Sorry, but you really need to stop trying so hard. It makes me very uncomfortable, and I'm sure Logan probably feels the same way."

After they hung up, Amelia knew she'd hurt her mother's feelings, but she didn't know what else to do. She'd tried to be less direct, but that obviously hadn't worked.

She plopped down on the sofa and stared at the wall. So here she was alone in her apartment, wondering what had caused Logan to turn away so abruptly after she thought everything was great between them. And now she'd upset her mother.

It took her a few minutes to finally come to the conclusion that she had to fix what she could and let the other go. She grabbed her purse and headed out the door to make amends with her mother.

Chapter 10

Logan worked hard with the crew laying the foundation for the new home they were building, but his mind kept darting back to the moment when Amelia had tried to kiss him. He felt awful for acting like he did, but after thinking things through, he was afraid of where their relationship was heading.

"Hey, Logan, what gives?" Andrew asked. "You're physically here, but it seems like your mind is miles away."

"Yeah, you're right."

"Girl problems?"

Logan hesitated and then nodded. "Something like that."

"Most girls I know like to talk things through. Have you thought about doing that?"

"I don't think it'll work this time."

"You must've done something really bad."

Andrew looked at him. "Or maybe it was her. Whatever the case, you're probably better off moping around for a while because you know as well as I do that moping will solve everything."

Andrew's sarcasm made Logan laugh. "Am I that bad?"

Andrew made an apologetic face and nodded. "Afraid so. If I didn't know you as well as I do, I wouldn't have come anywhere near you based on how you've been acting today."

"Sorry. I suppose it would be a good idea to talk to her about it, but it's just hard, ya know?"

"Anything worthwhile can be hard, but if there is any hope to resolve whatever is going on, you need to talk about it."

"There are some things I don't like to talk about."

"I totally understand," Andrew said. "We're guys. We'd rather just stay silent and mope …" He smiled. "… than talk about anything that makes us uncomfortable and let the women try to figure it out. But no matter how smart they might be, they can't read our minds."

"She doesn't need to read my mind. I think it would probably be better for both her and me to let this thing go and maybe stay from each other for a while."

Andrew scrunched his face. "I wasn't going to say this, but based on what you just said, I have to. It's going to be impossible for you to stay away from each other since you're both working on these projects."

"You know who she is?"

Andrew chuckled. "Yeah, me and everyone else who has seen the way you and Amelia look at each other. There is some serious chemistry between you two."

Logan pursed his lips. "I had no idea it showed."

"It doesn't just show. It zings." Andrew patted Logan on the back. "Why don't you head on over to her place now and talk to her? You've done everything you can here, and now we have to wait for the inspection before we proceed."

"Okay, I'll do that. Thanks for calling me out on my moodiness."

"Any time. After all, what's a friend for?"

Logan hopped into his truck and took off for Amelia's apartment. He didn't see her car in the parking lot, but maybe she'd put it somewhere else. So he went up to her door and knocked. No answer. He tried again. Still, no answer.

He pulled out his phone and started to punch in her number, but he stopped. He had no business trying to track her down. This could wait. He'd try again tomorrow. In fact, he'd go to her church. He knew she usually went to the late service, and she helped out with the Bible study, so he'd go to both.

Logan made some calls to a few of his buddies to let them know he was going to the main church. And to keep them from jumping to conclusions, he let them know he was doing it to square things up with a girl. They all understood that without question.

*

Amelia had no intention of going into detail about what had happened with Logan, but her mother pulled it out of her. "I was starting to think you made a good match, but something obviously short-circuited between last night and today." Her mother frowned. "What you just told me doesn't sound like Logan. He's usually pretty straightforward. I can't imagine him brooding like that."

"Oh, he was more than brooding."

Her mother picked up her phone. "Let me give him a call. I'll see what I can—"

"No." Amelia placed her hand on the phone. "You've done your part. Now it's my turn to take over. I'll get him to talk to me. I obviously said or did something to upset him, so it's my place to fix things."

"Okay, fair enough. But you do realize he'll be here on Monday morning to work on the house, right?"

"I know, but I'll be in school, so I can't be here."

"I wouldn't want you to, Amelia. If you're here, he won't be able to get a lick of work done." Her mother smiled. "This will all work out somehow."

Amelia wished she could be as certain as her mother, but the way he acted let her know it wouldn't be that simple. "I'd really like to see him before the weekend is over."

"Well …" Her mother tapped her chin with her

index finger. "You know where he goes to church, right?"

"That's right! I've always wanted to check out some of the satellite churches."

"This is your big chance. You can check out the church while you look for Logan." Her mother pulled her in for a hug. "Are you staying for dinner?"

"I don't think so." Amelia looked at the time on her cell phone and put it back in her pocket. "I need to go grocery shopping now. I don't have a thing in my fridge or pantry."

"You can take some stuff from here—"

"Thanks but no thanks. I want to buy my own groceries."

Her mother chuckled beneath her breath. "You've always been so independent and headstrong, but I reckon that's a good thing. Call me if you need anything, okay?"

"Will do."

With a plan in mind, Amelia felt like she'd at least have some answers by tomorrow. Even if it wasn't something she wanted to hear, she needed to know where she stood with Logan.

She stopped off at the grocery store on the way home and stocked up on what she'd need for the next week. By the time she went to bed, she was exhausted and fell right to sleep.

The next morning, she got up, said a prayer for guidance, had a cup of coffee, and took off for the satellite church that Logan attended. The sun was a bright spot in the middle of an ocean-blue sky with a few puffy white clouds that seemed to smile down at her.

When she walked in the door of the sanctuary, she noticed that although it wasn't as large as the main church, there were still quite a few people, and that might make it difficult to find Logan. So she decided to ask around.

The first guy she asked pointed to someone a few feet away. "I know Logan, but I haven't seen him. That's Nick, one of his Bible study buddies over there. See if he knows."

Amelia approached the second guy and asked him. He nodded. "Yeah, he won't be here today. He's met a girl, and he said he was going to her church this morning. But you're welcome to hang out with the group."

"Um …" A wave of nausea flooded Amelia. No way could she stay in the building, feeling like this. "Not today, but thanks."

He smiled and reached out to shake her hand. "Oh, by the way, I'm Nick. And you are?"

"Amelia. Nice to meet you Nick."

"Next time I see Logan I'll tell him you were here looking for him."

"Thanks."

As soon as Nick turned his back, she fled. Once she was in her car with the door closed, she dropped her head to the steering wheel and let the tears fall. She thought she and Logan had something special, but he obviously didn't waste a minute before finding someone else. She'd clearly misread his intentions. The very thought of him with another girl was so unfathomable after their kiss she couldn't imagine how she'd make it through the rest of the day without crumbling.

She was glad she'd moved out of her parents' house. Facing them at a time like this would be impossible. She drove to her apartment complex, parked her car, ran to her door, unlocked it and quickly went inside. The sunshine that had seemed so cheerful earlier was blinding and cloying, grating her last nerve. She needed darkness. To hide. To cry.

*

Logan walked into the classroom where the Bible study was about to be held. He looked around but didn't see Amelia. He saw the guy who led it last time he was there, so he started toward him, only to be intercepted by the same woman who'd introduced herself before.

"Remember me?" she said. "I'm Shay."

"Nice to see you, Shay. Have you seen Amelia?"

Shay frowned. "No, but sometimes she comes in right when it starts."

"Thanks." He took a step before turning around and grinning at her. "Good to see you again, Shay."

Shay gave him a closed-mouth smile, but she didn't make any more moves toward him. She clearly got the hint that he wasn't interested.

Throughout the Bible study, Logan glanced over his shoulder to look for Amelia. When it was over and she still hadn't shown up, he went out to the sanctuary to wait for her. He started to sit in the pew she'd chosen before, but he changed his mind and waited by the door. When the worship music started and she still wasn't there, he made the decision to leave. There was no way he'd be able to pay attention to the sermon, knowing what he had to do.

The problem was he had no idea how to do it. How could he apologize to the girl when he couldn't even find her?

He went out to the parking lot, got in his truck, and started to go home. But he decided to make a detour and drive by Amelia's apartment complex first.

And there was her car. He stopped beside it, thought for a moment, and then decided he was thinking way too much. He needed to act on his feelings and talk to the girl who'd stolen his every waking thought.

He parked his truck and went to her apartment door. After only a very brief hesitation, he pounded on the door. "Amelia, I need to talk to you."

Then he waited. He wasn't sure, but he thought he heard some movement inside, but she wasn't answering the door. He squeezed his eyes shut and asked the Lord for favor. *But only if it's Your will, Lord. I only want to do what You think is right for Amelia and me.*

He knocked on the door again, only this time more lightly. Then he became very still and listened. He was certain this time that someone was in there, so he decided to start talking now. Sure, he was taking a chance of making a fool of himself, but he'd already acted foolishly by acting the way he did.

"Amelia, I need to talk to you. It's extremely important." He paused. "I went to your church looking for you, but when you didn't show up, I decided to come back here looking for you." He waited again. The door remained closed. "Amelia, I think you and I have something special. I-I think I could easily fall in love with you ... that is, if I haven't already."

This was getting frustrating. He knew someone was in there, and who else could it be but Amelia? He decided to try one more time.

"Am—"

The door flung open, and there she was, all five-foot-something of a beautiful woman who had totally stolen his heart. She forced a smile, but he could tell that she'd been crying. Her eyes were puffy, and her cheeks were flushed.

"May I come in?"

She nodded and stepped aside. After he walked inside, she closed the door and turned around to face him.

"I hope you don't think I'm a stalker, but I went looking for you at your church. I sat through the Bible study, watching and waiting for you to come in, and then I went to the sanctuary door. When you didn't show up, I thought I'd lose my mind." He flinched as he saw the strange look on her face. "You think I'm being creepy, don't you?"

She giggled but quickly recovered. "Not creepy."

"Maybe stupid?"

She shook her head. "No, not creepy or stupid, because if you are, I am too. I went to your church looking for you."

"You did?"

She nodded. "I asked around and found out you'd met some girl and you were going to her church."

"You must have spoken to Chad or Nick."

"Nick."

"I called and told them I was going to church to see a very special girl." He tilted his head toward her. "And you are the girl I was talking about."

They stood in place looking at each other for several seconds. Finally, Amelia widened her stance and folded her arms. "What do we do now?"

"This." He reached for her and pulled her into his arms. "We need to talk, but I think we both need a kiss first."

Epilogue

(6 months later)

Amelia's mother's eyebrows slammed together. "Hold still, Amelia. I can't zip your dress if you don't stop fidgeting."

"Okay, sorry. It's just that I'm so nervous. I've never gotten married before."

"Of course you haven't." Her mother managed to get the zipper closed. "Turn around, sweetheart. I'd like to get a good look at you—my last look at my single daughter."

"Oh, Mama, you sound so dramatic."

A tear slid down her mother's cheek, and she quickly dabbed at it with the tissue she'd been holding. "I might sound dramatic to you, but it's a big moment for me. Are you sure you want to go through with this? I mean, it's not too late to change your mind."

"You have got to be kidding." Amelia half smiled, half glared at her mother. "You were the one who started this whole thing to begin with. I can't believe you're not doing cartwheels down the aisle."

Her mother grinned and tilted her head to the side as she sidestepped toward the door. "Yeah, you're right. I best be gettin' on out there. I love you, Amelia."

"I know you do, Mama. Love you too."

Once her mother left, Chelsea and Linea came back into the tiny bridal dressing room. "Are you ready?" Chelsea asked as she handed Amelia her bouquet.

Amelia nodded. "Let's get this show on the road."

As Amelia floated down the aisle toward the man she fell in love with the day she met him, she knew that God had worked a miracle in her life. Sure, He used her mother to get things started, but that didn't matter. No one had ever made her feel the way she felt at this very moment.

Her dad answered the pastor's question before handing her over to Logan who mouthed, "I love you," before turning around to face the pastor. Her heart hammered as they said their vows.

The rest of the ceremony was a blur. As they headed back up the aisle, she leaned over and whispered, "I'm glad you talked me into a videographer. I'm not even sure what just happened."

He laughed. "I'll tell you all about it after we get this reception over with. I can't wait to have you to myself."

She inhaled as they walked outside. The fresh scent of magnolias in bloom wafted through the air, and she saw that Logan noticed as well. But neither of them had to say a word to know it was a symbol of the sweetness of their love.

As soon as they got in the limo to go to the reception, Logan leaned over and laid a whopper of a kiss on her. She grinned. "That was nice. Do it again."

And he did.

Dear Reader,

I hope you enjoyed reading this story as much as I loved writing it. Please take a couple of minutes to leave an honest review on Amazon or Goodreads.

Thanks!

Debby Mayne

More books by Debby Mayne:

<u>Trouble in Paradise</u> **(contemporary romance – first book in the Belles in the City series)**

<u>Julia's Arranged Marriage</u> **(historical romance – first book in the Hollister Sisters Mail Order Brides series)**

<u>Murder Under the Mistletoe</u> **(mystery – first book in the Summer Walsh series)**

Printed in Great Britain
by Amazon